Good and Bad Luck

Reading practice

Words with <ck> and <qu>

<ck>	<qu>
back	quick
duck	quack
check	quest
pick	quiff
stick	quill
Mick	quit
rock	quench
luck	quilt
black	squid
smack	squint

Contents

Chapter 1: **Free Running** *Page 1*

Chapter 2: **Dognapped!** *Page 5*

Chapter 3: **Bring Floss Back!** *Page 7*

Chapter 4: **Good Luck and Bad Luck** *Page 9*

Vocabulary

free running	–	urban acrobatics, mostly interacting with city obstacles and environment
thud	–	a dull, heavy sound
plodded	–	walked slowly with heavy steps
bolted	–	ran away suddenly
thug	–	a violent person
shrubs	–	bushes
sprinted	–	ran at full speed over a short distance
mutt	–	a dog, especially a mongrel

Chapter 1: Free Running

"Mom, I want to go free running!" Abi said.

"Me too!" said Ben.

"That's OK, but you must have lessons. I'll check and pick a club," Mom said.

Mick ran a free-running club in the park. The kids had to do push-ups and sit-ups to get fit. Max wanted to quit. "You've got to stick at it!" Mick said.

"Jump from this rock – and land on both legs!" Mick yelled.

Max landed with a thud and fell on his back. "Just my luck!" he puffed.

"Quick, onto the wall!" Mick yelled.

Max jumped, SMACK, into the wall!

"*Onto* the wall, not *into* the wall!" Abi hissed.

Max picked himself up and jumped on.

"Good job! See you next lesson!" Mick said.

Chapter 2: Dognapped!

Abi spotted Miss Best as she huffed and puffed up the path. She had a bag packed with shopping. Miss Best stopped to rest. Then she picked the bag up and plodded on.

"Hello, Miss Best! Can we help you with that bag?" Abi asked Miss Best.

Just then, a man in a black jacket rushed up. He picked Floss up and ran.

Chapter 3: Bring Floss Back!

Floss yelped. Miss Best lifted her stick to whack the man, but he ducked. He bolted down the path. Floss yapped and snapped.

Miss Best was in shock. The kids jumped off the brick wall to help. "I'll get that thug!" Max yelled, but the man hopped onto a bike and sped off.

Chapter 4: Good Luck and Bad Luck

"Bring Floss back!" Ben yelled to Jet. Jet jumped over the shrubs and sprinted after the man. He was so quick, he ran as fast as the wind.

Jet ran next to the bike. The man kicked at him.

"Get off, mutt!" he yelled.

Jet jumped back. A black cab almost hit him. Jet kept on running.

Then a big truck stopped and blocked the traffic. The man on the bike was stuck. Jet jumped up and grabbed his leg. The bike rocked and the man fell off.

The man from the cab grabbed the thug. "Bad luck!" said the policeman and dragged him off. Jet had got Floss back. It was good luck for Miss Best!